First published in the United States, Great Britain, Canada, Australia,
and New Zealand in 2003 by North-South Books, an imprint
of Nord–Süd Verlag AG, Gossau Zürich, Switzerland.

Distributed in the United States by North-South Books Inc., New York

Library of Congress Cataloging–in–Publication Data is available.
A CIP catalogue record for this book is available from The British Library.

ISBN 0-7358-1845-2 (trade edition)
1 3 5 7 9 HC 10 8 6 4 2
ISBN 0-7358-1846-0 (library edition)
1 3 5 7 9 LE 10 8 6 4 2

Printed in Belgium

For more information about our books, and the authors and artists
who create them, visit our web site: www.northsouth.com

Meredith
and Her Magical Book of Spells

By Dorothea Lachner • Illustrated by Christa Unzner
Translated by J. Alison James

North–South Books
New York / London

It was a fine autumn morning in the witch village. Aside from the usual witchcraft in the air, everything seemed peaceful. Everything, that is, except Meredith the witch who was scolding her broomstick.

"Come back, you straw head, or I'll . . . I'll . . ." The problem was, Meredith had never been very good at magic. How would she ever catch her broom?

Suddenly Meredith heard an irritated snort.

It was Melusina Firebird, the eldest witch, flying past. She caught the disobedient broom. "It seems that I am always fixing your mistakes," she said. "But enough is enough. First thing in the morning, you will report to Professor Seventrix at the Witching School. Don't forget your book of spells."

The idea of spending day after day studying spells made Meredith's heart feel as dark as ink. Her spells always backfired, and she preferred to do things without magic anyway. She flew off reluctantly.

"School started weeks ago!" cried Helga, a witch with more eyes than teeth. "We're already on transformations."

Merle, who had a ring in her nose and an armband like a snake, hooted with laughter. "She won't be able to do anything. Look at her stinky old spell book! It's disgusting!"

Gruelda wrinkled her powder-white nose. "Pheeeeeww! I can smell it from here!"

All the others laughed.

Meredith's spell book rustled its pages, as if it were offended.

"Quiet!" Professor Seventrix shouted. "Or I'll start casting warts!" She turned to Meredith. "Pay attention, and if you need help, just ask Helga."

."Me? Help her? Baaaahhhh!" shrieked Helga. Thirteen green warts suddenly popped up on her nose.

Professor Seventrix took advantage of the sudden silence and began the lesson. "Animal Conjuring, Part One: We'll cover birds, snakes, toads, spiders, and other household pets. Let's begin with birds."

"Who can conjure a white raven?" asked Professor Seventrix. "I'll leave the room and when I return, I expect to see eight snowy–white ravens perched on my desk."

"No problem," Helga said. "Swirl a white feather three times–"

"Seven times!" argued Merle.

"You don't swirl!" Gruelda scoffed. There was a sudden explosion. It was *not* magic. Poking, kicking, spitting, clawing–it was a fight! Meredith watched in silence. She had no idea how to do the spell and wasn't about to ask those girls for help.

"Pssst! Meredith!" came a voice from the corner. She looked, but the only thing there was her book of spells. She didn't know it could talk. "They have mocked you. They have ridiculed me," the book muttered. "Let's show them what we can do."

It fluttered open to a cocoa-splattered, coffee-flecked page and Meredith whispered the spell that was written there. For a moment, nothing happened. Then a coffee-flecked, cocoa-splattered raven fluttered around the room, cawing loudly.

The girls looked shocked. Then they grinned.

"That's better than a boring old white raven!" cried Gruelda. Soon, all the witches were conjuring a wild assortment of birds that darted around the room, cawing and hooting and screeching.

Just then Professor Seventrix swept back in, startling the flock, which flew out of the window. "Nice work," she said. "But now that you have made them, you are responsible for them. Catch them, quickly, before they get away."

"How do we do that?" whined Helga. "Sprout wings and fly?" The birds were circling higher. There was no time to run to the broomstick shed.

"Ahem," muttered Meredith's spell book. It started fluttering its pages.

"Your book is so filthy," said Gruelda, sneering. "Look at all those crumbs."

"That's it!" cried Meredith. She shook the book and gave everyone a handful of crumbs. The girls leaned out of the window and coaxed the birds back.

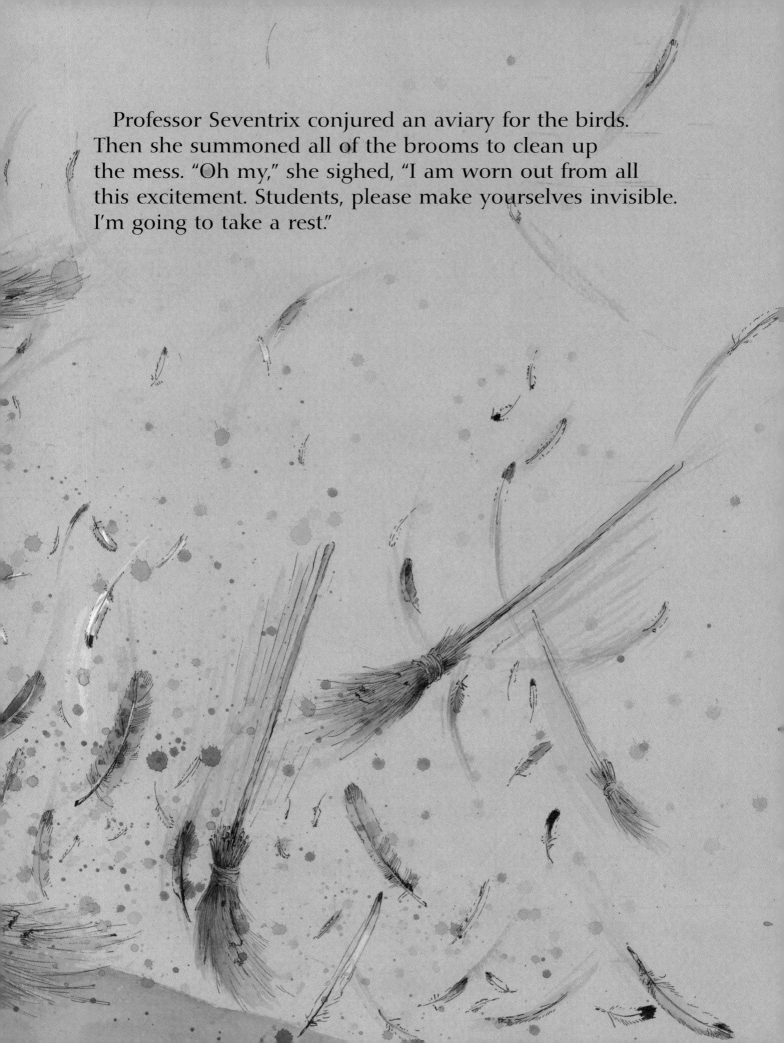

Professor Seventrix conjured an aviary for the birds.
Then she summoned all of the brooms to clean up
the mess. "Oh my," she sighed, "I am worn out from all
this excitement. Students, please make yourselves invisible.
I'm going to take a rest."

"But we haven't learned the invisibility spell yet!" said
Gruelda.

"Let's ask my book," Meredith suggested. She held it up
respectfully. "Could you please make us invisible?"

"Big . . . Bigger . . . BIGGEST!" said the book. With a rustle
of paper, it grew to the size of a tent. The students crawled
inside—totally hidden from their teacher. And there they
stayed, laughing and telling ghost stories.

Melusina Firebird dropped in for a visit just as Professor Seventrix woke from her rest. "Where are your students?" Melusina Firebird asked. "Has Meredith's muddled magic made the whole class disappear?"

Professor Seventrix smiled. "She certainly has no talent for spells. But look," she said, pointing to the class, "Meredith has turned a bunch of bickering witches into fast friends. That is *real* magic, if you ask me."

The book fluttered its pages. "Ahem."

Meredith stood up. "I wouldn't have been able to do a thing without my magical book of spells," she said.

Melusina Firebird beamed. "Well, who would have guessed?" she said. "Anyone with a book like that hardly needs lessons. Meredith can stick to her own kind of magic from now on and not worry about Witching School."

Meredith said good–bye to her new friends. "Come over sometime and I'll teach you how to build a birdhouse," she offered. "You use a hammer and nails and some glue instead of spells. It's fun!"

And with that, Meredith packed up her magical book of spells, hopped on to her broomstick, and happily headed home.